KNIGHTMARE

For Lucy, Theo and Tara – PB

STRIPES PUBLISHING
An imprint of Little Tiger Press
1 The Coda Centre, 189 Munster Road,
London SW6 6AW

A paperback original
First published in Great Britain in 2015

Text copyright © Peter Bently, 2015
Cover illustrations copyright © Fred Blunt, 2015
Illustrations copyright © Artful Doodlers, 2015

ISBN: 978-1-84715-509-2

Printed and bound in the UK.

10 9 8 7 6 5 4 3 2 1

KNIGHTMARE

Rotten Luck!

PETER BENTLY

Stripes

CEDRIC'S WORLD

CASTLE BOMBAST

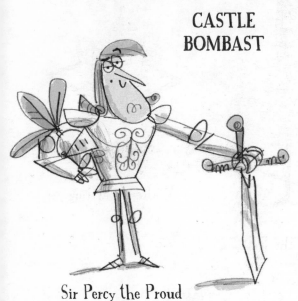

Sir Percy the Proud

Cedric
Thatchbottom
(Me!)

Patchcoat the Jester

Margaret the Cook

BLACKSTONE FORT

Sir Roland the Rotten

Walter Warthog

SPIFFINGTON MANOR

Algernon Whympleigh

Sir Spencer the Splendid

Chapter One
Birthday Bash

FLASH! RUMBLE! CRRR-ASH!

The thunderclap was so startling that
Sir Percy jumped and I snapped off the
button I was doing up on his evening tunic.
Patchcoat the jester dropped all his juggling
balls. (He was practising a new trick that
seemed to involve throwing the balls into
the air and *not* catching them.)

BOOM! BOOM! BOOM!

We all jumped again. It took us a moment to realize that it wasn't the storm this time. Someone was knocking at the door of our cramped and smelly guest chamber. The knock came again and the door slowly opened with a creak.

Standing in the doorway was a tall, heavily built man with a long scar on his cheek and a nose that looked like he'd had an argument with a battering ram.

KNIGHTMARE

"The banquet's about to be served," he scowled. "'Urry up." He turned and lumbered back out into the corridor, slamming the door behind him. We heard him bashing on the doors of the other guest chambers as he went.

"Charming chap, that deputy sheriff, isn't he?" said Patchcoat.

We had encountered him once before. He'd greeted us when we arrived that afternoon in the pouring rain. Well, I say "greeted" but he'd just pointed at the stairs and muttered, "Another lot fer the sheriff to feed? Top floor, third door along. Plenty o' room fer the three of you. And mind yer don't drip on the furniture."

"I jolly well won't let him spoil my

evening," said Sir Percy. "I do love a
royal birthday party! I wonder who else
is coming? Sir Spencer I suppose. And
probably Sir Roland, too. Oh well, never
mind."

Even the thought of seeing his arch-
enemy, Sir Roland the Rotten, didn't sour
Sir Percy's mood. The king had invited
all his knights and nobles to celebrate his
birthday with a weekend of banquets and
boar hunting in the forest of Grimwood.
We were staying at Fleecingham Castle,
on the far side of the forest, as guests of
the new sheriff of Fleecingham – Earl
Crawleigh de Creepes.

Sir Percy had immediately ordered a

load of fancy new gear. New boots and tights, a green velvet tunic, complete with hat, plus a plume and a fancy gold peacock brooch to hold it in place.

I was almost as excited as my master. A weekend hunting with the king! I was bound to get a chance to do some of the proper knight stuff that Sir Percy was always forgetting to teach me. I couldn't wait!

"Righty-ho, chaps," Sir Percy said, once I'd stitched his button back on. "Off we go! It's party time!"

We followed him out into the dark, chilly corridor. It was lit by a feeble candle that sputtered in the wind blowing through a large crack in the wall.

"I hope the weather isn't this bad tomorrow," I said to Patchcoat. "I'd hate it if the king cancelled the hunt. And I don't think I could bear spending all day in this miserable castle!"

"Wasn't always like this, you know," said Patchcoat, who was practising his juggling trick as we walked along. "One of the stable lads told me it was a much more cheerful place when the last sheriff was around. Whoops!"

"You mean the sheriff who wanted to overthrow the king?" I said, as Patchcoat stopped to pick up his balls. "The one who fled abroad before the king's men could arrest him – Sir Edward Whatshisname?"

"Worthington," said Patchcoat. "That's him, Ced. Very popular guy, apparently, despite being a traitor. Nice to the staff, threw lots of parties, that sort of thing. Castle was filled with colourful paintings and tapestries. But this new sheriff is a total skinflint. No more merry parties. Flogged off all the decorations. *And* he sacked half the staff and cut

13

everyone else's wages to pay for a load of new soldiers. The stable lad reckons he's obsessed with catching some masked robber called the Ghost."

I was about to ask Patchcoat more about the robber when the door of another guest room opened and out stepped Sir Spencer with his squire, Algernon. They were dressed in matching turquoise and orange satin tunics plus cloaks of green velvet with a gold trim.

"Evening, Spencer," said Sir Percy, eyeing his friend's outfit rather enviously. "Looking forward to the party?"

"Evening, Perce," beamed Sir Spencer, shaking back his golden curls. "Couldn't miss a chance to wish His Maj a happy birthday, could we, Algie?"

Or show off your wardrobe, I thought.

Before Algernon could answer, another door opened. This time it was the beefy, bearded figure of Sir Roland, along with his sneaky squire, Walter Warthog.

"Well, well, well, look who it is," said Sir Roland. "I might have known you two prancing peacocks wouldn't miss a free banquet, eh, Walter? Hur-hur-hur!"

"And a jolly good evening to you, too, Roland," said Sir Percy. "At least *we've* made an effort with our clothes. Is that an *egg stain* on your tunic, by any chance?"

"Why, you—" Sir Roland growled.

KNIGHTMARE

"N-now, no arguing, chaps," said Sir Spencer hastily, as we reached the stairs down to the great hall. "It wouldn't do to arrive at the king's birthday dinner making a scene, would it?"

Sir Roland glared at Sir Percy, but held his tongue.

"I say!" declared Sir Spencer suddenly. "Bagsy I sit next to the king!"

"Oh *yes*, Sir Spencer," simpered Algernon. "He'll definitely want the most *elegant* knight sitting next to him."

"Rubbish!" said Walter. "The king'll want the most *fearless* knight. And that's *my* master!"

"Well, *I* think it ought to be *me*," said Sir Percy airily. "After all, *who* defeated Sir Roland in the king's tournament?"

Actually that would be me, I thought.

The three knights stopped in their tracks. For a moment they just stood there, eyeing one another. And then, all of a sudden, they bolted.

"Me first, losers!" hollered Sir Roland.

"No, me!"

"Me!"

As the three knights charged down the stairs, Walter shoved past me and Patchcoat.

"Outta my way, Fatbottom!" he yelled. "Go on, Sir Roland, you can do it!"

"Watch out!" cried Patchcoat. His juggling balls flew out of his hands, and bounced down the stairs.

It all happened in an instant.

Sir Spencer slipped on a ball, squealed and grabbed Sir Percy. My master lost his balance, sending the two of them tumbling head first.

"AARGH!"

"WAAH!"

"I win!" Sir Roland cackled gleefully, as he reached for the handle of the door. "I'm going to sit next to the king! Nah-nah-nee-nah-n-*OOF*!"

Sir Spencer and Sir Percy slammed into Sir Roland, and the three of them barrelled through the door and rolled to a halt in a heap of tangled limbs.

"You idiots!" roared Sir Roland. "You pair of total—"

"Now, look here," came the muffled voice of my master. "That was your silly squire's fault, Roland. If he hadn't—"

"I've ripped my tunic!" wailed Sir Spencer.

But before the three knights could start squabbling and bickering again, a voice said, "Ahem!"

Standing over them, looking VERY cross, were King Fredbert and Queen Malicia. And that wasn't all. Seated at a long banqueting table was just about every lord, lady and knight for miles around.

Chapter Two

Banquet Bombshell

"Your Majesties!" grinned Sir Percy, freeing his face from Sir Roland's armpit. "How simply *splendid* to see you both. And happy birthday, sire! I trust all is well with Your Majesty?"

"Fine, thanks," said the king. "Which is more than can be said for the sheriff."

"Oh dear, dear," schmoozed Sir Percy.

KNIGHTMARE

"I'm *awfully* sorry to hear that, Your Majesty. Has he been taken ill?"

The queen frowned. "No," she said. "You're sitting on him."

There was a groan from underneath the knot of knights. They hastily untangled themselves to reveal a little man with a pointy beard and thin moustache. The deputy sheriff ran to help him up.

"Thundewing thumbscwews!" shrieked the sheriff. "Of all the dimwitted, dunderheaded, dog-bwained—"

"Sorry, sir," grunted the deputy sheriff.

"Not you, Lurk!" the sheriff snapped. He pointed at the three knights. "These fools. Why, I've a good mind to lock 'em all up and thwow away the key!"

The king laid a hand on his shoulder. "Come along, sheriff! We'd better sit down," he said. "They're about to serve dinner!"

"Vewy well, Your Majesty," he said. "But these oafs haven't heard the last of this!"

The sheriff strutted to his seat beside

the king's throne with as much dignity as he could muster.

Queen Malicia turned to the knights. "And as for *you* three," she hissed. "After that little scene, you can jolly well sit in the corner."

She pointed to the end of the table furthest from the king. Sir Percy, Sir Spencer and Sir Roland sheepishly squeezed themselves on to the end of the bench next to a large baroness.

The queen took her throne beside the king. "Happy birthday, Fredbert dear!" she declared.

And then she led the whole hall in a rousing chorus:

KNIGHTMARE

"For he's a jolly good monarch!
For he's a jolly good monarch!
For he's a jolly good monarch!
And so say all of us!"

"Thank you!" beamed the king, after all the cheering and clapping had died down. Then the kitchen door opened and in marched a procession of servants carrying a peacock pie, a whole roast boar and dozens of other steaming dishes.

I served up Sir Percy's food and stood behind him while he cheerfully stuffed his face. Sir Roland was still sulking as he chewed noisily on a haunch of boar, while Sir Spencer just picked at his food and kept

KNIGHTMARE

whining to Algernon about his torn tunic. I'll say one thing about my master, he never stays grumpy for long.

After the main course, there was another round of cheers as a magnificent birthday cake topped with a marzipan crown was brought in. I served Sir Percy a large slice. He had just stuffed in an enormous mouthful when the queen

raised her hand for silence.

"My lords, ladies and knights," she declared. "You may now give the king his presents!"

Sir Percy suddenly coughed and spluttered violently, spraying cake all over the tablecloth and the elderly earl sitting opposite, who had dozed off with his mouth wide open.

Sir Percy covered his face with a napkin and turned to me with a look of pure panic.

"Cedric!" he whispered. "This is a disaster. I've forgotten to get the king a present! Why didn't you remind me?"

I could have said, "Because I was too busy trying to remember all the things you'd got for yourself." But that would have been a breach of the Squire's Code about being sarky to your master.

All eyes had turned to our end of the table, where Sir Roland and Sir Spencer were already producing gifts from inside their tunics.

"Aha!" said the king brightly. "I see Sir Percy is *dying* to go first. Come on, then,

Percy, show us what've you brought me!"

"Ah, yes, well, sire, I – um – er…" my master gibbered. "You see, er, my *squire* here…"

Then I had a brainwave. Wherever Sir Percy went, he made sure I packed at least one signed copy of *The Song of Percy*, his best-selling book, to give to his admirers. It's full of thrilling stories about his brave deeds. The only snag is that they are all ever so slightly made up.

"Um – I left it upstairs, Your Majesty," I said quickly.

"You did?" said Sir Percy. "Um – I mean, he did, sire!"

"Silly boy!" said the king with a chuckle.

"You'd better go and fetch it then, hadn't you?"

"Yes, Your Majesty," I said.

"And I hope it's not another signed copy of your book, Sir Percy," said the king. "You've sent me ten already!"

Everyone roared with laughter. Yikes! Now what was I going to do? But before I could think of a Plan B there was a noise at the door and a breathless peasant came running into the hall.

"Yer Majesties! Yer Majesties!" he panted, doffing his cap.

The sheriff shot to his feet. "What is the meaning of this outwage!" he cried. "How dare you intewwupt the

KNIGHTMARE

king's birthday party!
Lurk, thwow this wepulsive
peasant out at once!"

"Yes, Yer Lordship,"
grunted Lurk. He lumbered
towards the peasant, cracking
his knuckles menacingly.

"Hold on," said the queen. "The poor
fellow looks all hot and bothered. Perhaps
we'd better hear what he has to say."

"Quite right, Malicia, dear," the king
agreed. "It might be important. Do sit
down, sheriff."

The sheriff bowed stiffly and sat down,
fiddling with his moustache and glowering
at the peasant.

"I've been robbed!" the peasant began. "By bandits!"

"Bandits?" thundered the king. "Good heavens! Where?"

"On me way 'ome through the forest, Yer Majesty," said the peasant. "I sold three goats an' a goose in the market today and made a nice little pile o' cash. Them robbers took the 'ole blinkin' lot!"

"What did they look like?" asked the queen.

"Dunno, Yer Majesty," said the peasant. "Most of 'em had 'oods. And their leader was wearin' a mask!"

"The Ghost of Gwimwood!" cried the sheriff. "I thought as much!"

KNIGHTMARE

"*Ghost?*" the king frowned. "Sheriff, are you seriously suggesting this man was robbed by a *ghost?*"

"No, sire," replied the sheriff. "Not a ghost but *the* Ghost. The leader of a notowious band of outlaws who live in the fowest. They call him the Ghost because he always vanishes without a twace. But I'll catch him one day, sire. And when I do, ooh! What fun I'll have!" He rubbed his hands together gleefully. "We haven't had a decent *execution* awound here for ages. The last shewiff was such a tewwible *softie*, you see…"

"Sir Edward Worthington, a softie?" said the king. "I'm surprised to hear that, sheriff."

The sheriff looked a bit flummoxed. "Ah, well, yes of course Sir Edward was a dweadful *twaitor*, sire," he said. "That letter I found pwoved it. But he didn't like chopping people's heads off. I shall change all that. Starting with the Ghost!"

"Um – beggin' yer pardon, Yer Majesty," said the peasant. "But I don't reckon it *were* the Ghost who robbed me."

"What makes you so sure?" asked the king.

"For starters, the Ghost and his band *never* rob us peasants." The peasant looked rather nervously round the hall. "He only robs – beggin' everybody's pardon – posh folks."

34

KNIGHTMARE

There were gasps of alarm. Sir Spencer gave a little squeak.

"Good gracious," said the king. "Do you mean to say we could all have been robbed on the way here? Why didn't you warn us, sheriff?"

The sheriff shifted uneasily in his seat. "I – er – didn't want to *alarm* you, sire," he said.

"Oh, the Ghost don't rob *all* posh people, Yer Majesty," said the peasant, trying not to catch the sheriff's eye. "Only them that is good pals of the sheriff's."

The sheriff scowled but said nothing.

"And another thing," the peasant went on. "The Ghost is always nice and polite, even when 'e's robbin' folks. The blokes

that robbed me was rude an' unfriendly.
They even scoffed the pasty the wife made
me as a snack. The Ghost would never do
anything like that."

"Wubbish!" snapped the sheriff.
"Who else could it have been? Sire, I
think we've heard enough!" He nodded
to Lurk, who seized the peasant and

frogmarched him to the
door. "If you ask me,
these wotten peasants
deserve to be wobbed.
I've offered a
fat weward but
they do nothing
to help me catch

WANTED
Dead or Alive
The Ghost of Grimwood
Reward £100
by order of
The Sheriff

the Ghost! They wegard him as some kind of *hewo*! Perhaps if Your Majesty were to let me double their taxes? And maybe do a couple of *teensy-weensy* little *executions*? That would teach them a lesson!"

"Beg pardon, Yer Majesty," said the peasant, as Lurk thrust him out of the hall. "We just can't afford all these taxes the sheriff makes us pay. I know they say Sir Edward was a traitor, but at least he was fair!"

"The fellow's right, sheriff," said the king. "If you put taxes up any more we'll have a rebellion on our hands. I can't allow it."

"Balderdash!" snarled the sheriff. "Tax 'em and axe 'em, I say!"

"Calm down, sheriff," said the king. "I can't be doing with rebellious peasants. And I certainly don't want any more robberies in the forest. There's only one thing for it. If you can't catch this Ghost chappie yourself, my brave knights will have to do it. Tomorrow one of them can miss the boar hunt and search for the Ghost of Grimwood instead."

"Wh-what?" said Sir Spencer. "You mean ride into the f-forest alone, sire?"

"Precisely, Sir Spencer," said the king. His eyes swept around the table. "Now, who's going to volunteer, eh? Kindly stand up!"

KNIGHTMARE

There was an awkward silence. Sir Percy was suddenly fascinated by the carved gargoyles on the ceiling. Sir Spencer became engrossed with a tiny bit of fluff on his sleeve.

I can't say I blamed them. Grimwood is big and dark and scary. If the Ghost and his outlaws lived there, they must be a pretty terrifying bunch.

The only knight who wasn't desperately trying to avoid the king's eye was Sir Roland.

"Bunch of wimps!" I heard him mutter. "If they won't volunteer, I will!"

He was starting to stand up when the elderly earl opposite suddenly woke with such a start that he knocked over his goblet of mead. The mead flew across the table and splashed straight into Sir Percy's lap.

"Bother!" he yelped, jumping to his feet. "I'm soaked! Cedric, go and fetch me a clo—"

He trailed off as he realized that everyone was staring at him.

"Bravo, Sir Percy!" declared the king. "Well done for volunteering. You will leave for Grimwood at dawn."

Chapter Three
Forest Fiasco

I was up well before sunrise the next morning to get everything ready for Sir Percy's mission, including scrabbling together a picnic from some leftovers down in the castle kitchens. By the time I woke my master, the sun was already peeping over the forest. It didn't look quite so scary in the daylight and at least it had

stopped raining. But I was still glad when
Sir Percy decided to bring Patchcoat, too.

"He can tell us a few jokes as we go
along," Sir Percy said, as we stepped
out into the castle courtyard. The king,
queen and sheriff were getting ready to
go hunting with Sir Spencer and the other
knights. "Besides, it's always useful to
have an extra pair of eyes when one is
hunting for dangerous outlaws, don't you
think?"

My master was in a remarkably
confident mood. Even so, I was surprised
when he turned down the king's offer of a
platoon of his best soldiers.

"Are you sure, Sir Percy?" said the king.

"Quite sure, sire," said Sir Percy. "Any extra men will only – um – make too much noise. *Stealth*, sire, that's the only way to catch the Ghost. Creep up on him unawares, that sort of thing."

"What?" said the sheriff sharply. "Do you sewiously expect to catch the Ghost with only a *squire* and a *jester?*"

"Of course, sheriff," my master replied. "Don't forget that I once captured Filbert the Fox and his gang single-handedly. It's in *The Song of Percy.*"

"Happy now, sheriff?" said the king. "It's about time we were off. The early bird catches the boar, eh?"

"Actually, sire, if you'll excuse me I

think I'll miss today's hunt," said the
sheriff. "I've just wemembered I've some
urgent business away fwom the castle."

"Really, sheriff?" said the king. "Why
didn't you mention it before? Very well, if
it's important I suppose you'll have to go.
All the more boar for me!"

The sheriff bowed and hurried back
into the castle, just as Sir Roland came
out in full hunting gear, with Walter
struggling under the weight of a massive
crossbow.

"Good luck, Sir Percy," said the king,
clapping my master on the back. "I wish
all my knights were as brave and fearless
as you!"

Sir Roland gave a little snort of laughter.
Unfortunately the king heard him.

"What's so funny, Sir Roland?" he
frowned.

"*You*, sire!" said Sir Roland. "I mean no,
er, I—"

"*Me?*" snapped the king.

"No-no-no, sire," mumbled Sir
Roland, blushing. "What I meant was
I-I-I—"

"So you think I'm here to *amuse* you, do you, Sir Roland?" said the king. "Like some kind of *jester*, eh?"

Sir Percy was biting his lip to stop himself laughing. He was clearly enjoying watching Sir Roland squirm.

"Well, Sir Roland, unlike Master Patchcoat here I *don't* enjoy being laughed at," said the king. "*You* can jolly well stay behind and guard the castle!"

The king strode off to join the queen at the head of the hunting party. For a moment Sir Roland stood there gawping. Then, with a furious look at Sir Percy, he stomped back to the castle.

"We'll get you for this, Fatbottom,"

hissed Walter. "That's if the Ghost of Grimwood doesn't get you first!"

We followed the royal hunting party out of the castle. Sir Percy, whistling merrily, led the way on Prancelot while Patchcoat and I rode on Gristle.

"The king's got a point," said Patchcoat. "Even if we're quiet and stealthy like Sir Percy says, does he seriously reckon the three of us can capture the Ghost and his band? They're bound to put up a fight, aren't they?"

"I know," I said with a shiver. "Sir Percy's being very jolly, considering."

"A bit *too* jolly, if you ask me, Ced."

Uh-oh. Was my master up to something?

As we passed through the town gates, I noticed a couple of peasants at the side of the road – a short stocky man with a staff, and a tall skinny youth with a bow. I could have sworn that the stocky one gave the youth a nudge and a nod in our direction. A little further up the road I glanced round to see the two peasants walking behind us. I thought of mentioning it to Patchcoat, but the next time I looked they had both disappeared.

We were just at the point where the main road entered the forest.

KNIGHTMARE

"Right, this path should do nicely,"
said Sir Percy, veering on to a rough track.
"Follow me, chaps!"

I watched the hunting party carry on
along the road without us.

"Um – are you sure this is the best way,
Sir Percy?" I said, pointing to a signpost
half hidden by bushes.

BEWARE!
HERE BE MONSTERS
AND BEASTIES.
ENTER AT
YOUR PERIL!

No wonder those two peasants had stopped following us.

"No need to worry, dear boy!" said Sir Percy. "We won't go far into the forest. We'll just trot along this path for a while until we find some charming little glade among the trees. Then we'll have our picnic and maybe a snooze in the sun for a few hours before trotting back to the castle in good time for supper."

"But — but what about tracking down the Ghost, Sir Percy?" I said.

"Oh, *that*," said my master breezily. "Well, we'll keep an eye out for the fellow, of course. But let's be realistic, Cedric. The forest stretches for miles. Do you seriously think we have a chance of bumping into *anyone*, let alone the Ghost? His Majesty won't be at all surprised if we *don't* find the Ghost. So we might as well relax and enjoy our little jaunt, eh?"

So that was it! Sir Percy had no intention whatsoever of tracking down the Ghost. No wonder he was cheerful. And no wonder he didn't want any of the king's soldiers coming with us!

Patchcoat gave me a wry grin. "Oh well," he said, as we headed down the track. "At least it means we won't actually have to fight the Ghost and his gang."

"That's true," I said. "But it also means I've missed out on the hunt. I might *finally*

have had a go with a bow and arrow!"

We followed Sir Percy as he looked for a spot to stop for a picnic. But as we got deeper into the forest, the trees started to grow closer and closer together.

"Bother!" said Sir Percy. "There must be a clearing somewhere. We'll just have to keep looking."

In the gloom the trees took on weird shapes and I began to make out spooky faces in their gnarled and twisted trunks.

"I don't know about you," I said to Patchcoat. "But this place gives me the willies... Eek! What's that?"

As if on cue, a strange creature had dropped down out of the trees right in

front of us. I realized that it was a plump
man with the longest, bushiest and whitest
beard I had ever seen. It covered his whole
body, right down to his knobbly knees.
Which was just as well, because he was
also stark, staring butt-naked.

"Brother Dermot's the name," said the
man. "I'm a tree hermit."

"A tree hermit?" said Sir Percy.

"That's right," said Brother Dermot. "Anyhow, there I was sittin' in my tree, mindin' me own business like, when I sees you lot wandering along. So I thinks, better hop down and *warn* 'em, see?"

"W-warn us about what?" said Sir Percy.

"Oh, *nothing*," said Dermot. "It usually sleeps at this time of day, anyway."

"*What* does?" said Sir Percy.

"The Man-Eatin' Monster of Grimwood," said Dermot, matter-of-factly. "It *loves* humans, see. 'Specially nice tasty *tinned* ones! Not to mention fresh juicy jesters. And *boys*. That's why I live up a tree. Much safer up there, see!"

KNIGHTMARE

"Well, my dear fellow, it's, er, time we were off," said Sir Percy. "As a matter of fact we only planned to come *exactly* this far before turning back to the castle. Isn't that right, Cedric?"

"Er, yes, Sir Percy," I lied. First I'd heard of it, but I wasn't arguing.

"Hold on," said Patchcoat suspiciously. "How come no one at the castle mentioned this Man-Eating Monster thingy?"

The hermit hesitated for a moment. Then he said, "That's because no one who's seen it ever went home to tell the tale! Now, I'll show you a shortcut back to the castle." He pointed at a tree just ahead. "Right after that chestnut tree there's a fork in the path, right?"

"Right," nodded Sir Percy.

"Take the left fork," said Dermot. "*Not* the right. Right?"

"Um – right," said Sir Percy quickly. "Thank you. Now I think we'd better get a move on. Good day, Brother Dermot!"

"Cheerio!" said Brother Dermot. He turned and, with a flash of his hairy bottom, disappeared up a tree.

We soon reached the fork in the path. But then we hit a snag. Try as we might, Patchcoat and I just couldn't convince Sir Percy to take the left fork.

"We're sure the hermit said go *left*, Sir Percy," I pleaded.

"Nonsense," said Sir Percy. "I hope you're not forgetting your Squire's Code and arguing with your master, Cedric. Did he or did he not say 'Right after the chestnut tree'?"

"Well, *yes*," I admitted. "But *then* he said—"

"Exactly," Sir Percy interrupted. "No more arguing. Follow me!"

Patchcoat and I looked at each other as Sir Percy galloped off.

"Don't worry, Ced," said Patchcoat. "He'll soon realize this isn't the way. Then we'll just turn round and come back."

"I hope so," I sighed. "That's if we're not eaten by a monster first!"

Chapter Four

Bear Scare

"Can't be far now!" said Sir Percy for the umpteenth time.

It was three hours later and we had stopped for a late picnic lunch. So late, in fact, that it was nearly dinner. Unfortunately, my master still showed no sign of turning back.

"We're almost there, you mark my

words," he said, swallowing the last of his cold peacock pie. "In fact, we'd see the castle by now if this dashed forest weren't in the way."

I doubted that. Not only was there no sign of the castle, there was no sign of anything at all. Except trees, trees and more trees.

As we set off again I realized the light was starting to fade. It was getting harder to see the path in front of us. If that wasn't bad enough, the branches were really low, so we had to dismount and lead Prancelot and Gristle by the reins.

"I must say I'm looking forward to a nice *hot* dinner," said Sir Percy. "I wonder how much further it is."

"Look!" I said, squinting in the gloom. "There's someone on the path ahead! They might know, Sir Percy."

"So there is," said Sir Percy. "I say, you there!" he hollered. "Is it far to the castle?"

The person had his back to us and he didn't turn round. His only reply was a surly grunt.

"How rude!" muttered Sir Percy. "Obviously another of these woodland loner types. Woodcutter or somesuch."

He tried once more. "My good fellow, I asked you a simple question. Is it far to the castle?"

But the figure just grunted again. It was

hard to tell in the twilight, but he appeared to be heavily built and wearing some kind of thick overall and hat.

"Now look here," harrumphed Sir Percy. "I am Sir Percy Piers Peregrine de Bluster de Bombast and I will *not* be addressed in that impolite manner. Will you *kindly* answer my question?"

The answer was a growl followed by a loud, bloodcurdling ROAR!

"We'll take that as a *no* then," said Patchcoat, as the stranger slowly turned round.

Uh-oh. "That's no woodcutter, Sir Percy," I said. "That's a BEAR! RUN FOR IT!"

KNIGHTMARE

ROARRRR!

"Aargh!"

"Yikes!"

"Eek!"

Prancelot and Gristle bolted into the trees. And we weren't far behind, running like crazy with the bear crashing through the undergrowth in hot pursuit.

KNIGHTMARE

I blundered blindly through the dark forest, tripping over roots and ivy and being walloped by branches. I was falling further and further behind. Eventually I had to stop and catch my breath.

So this is it, I thought. *I'm never going to be a knight. I'm going to be a bear's bedtime snack instead!*

I waited for the bear to appear. Nothing. Either we'd given the bear the slip or it had changed its mind about having us as a tasty three-course meal.

"Sir Percy! Patchcoat! Stop!" I called. "The bear's gone!"

I ran and caught up with them.

"Excellent!" said Sir Percy, between

gasps for breath. "I knew my – um – plan would work!"

"Plan, Sir Percy?" I asked.

"Indeed, my plan to, er, bamboozle the bear by – um – leading it into unfamiliar territory," he panted. "Very useful tactic for, er, er – confusing an enemy, Cedric!"

A tactic otherwise known as running for your life like a gibbering crazy person, I thought.

Hearing a soft whinnying in the bushes nearby, Patchcoat and I went to fetch Prancelot and Gristle.

"First a monster and now a bear!" said Patchcoat. "This sure is one scary forest, Ced!"

"Too right," I agreed. "But at least we haven't had to face the Ghost and his gang yet."

"Right, chaps," said Sir Percy, when we returned. "That's quite enough adventure for one day. It's dinner and bed for me! Let's get back on the path."

"Er, just one little question, Sir Percy," I said. "Where exactly *is* the path?"

"Well, it's *this* way, of course," said Sir Percy, striding ahead. "Ah, no, hold on, it's – it's—" He stopped in his tracks.

We'd run a long way and in the darkness it was impossible to remember which direction we'd come from. We were lost, at night, in the middle of Grimwood.

"We shall simply have to set up camp," said Sir Percy. "We must make a fire and find ourselves something to eat. It'll all be rather jolly."

He sat down on a tree stump. "So, while you two chaps get on with those little jobs," he said, "I'll take full responsibility for – um – keeping guard."

As usual I'd be doing the dirty work, but at least I had Patchcoat to help me. And he happened to have a tinderbox in his jester's bag, so making the fire turned out to be easy. Once the blaze was going, I thought about finding food. But what?

KNIGHTMARE

It was the wrong time of year for berries and nuts.

Sir Percy had nipped behind a tree for a tinkle. Suddenly he started to yelp.

"Ow! Ooh! Ow! Ah! Cedric, help! Ow!"

"What is it, Sir Percy?" I said, running over.

"A dockleaf, Cedric, quickly!" he winced. "I've – *ouch* – stung myself."

Sir Percy had accidentally blundered

into a patch of nettles in the dark. While
I was fetching him some dockleaves, I
remembered that my mum often made
dockleaf soup. I gave him the leaves then
went to collect some more in a pot from
Gristle's saddlebag. After picking off all
the slugs, I filled the pot with water from
a nearby stream and put it on the fire.
Before long we were taking it in turns
to sip the thick green soup straight
from the pot.

"Thank you, Cedric," said Sir Percy.
"Rather dull peasant fare, but at least
you tried to liven it up with one or two
mushrooms."

"Mushrooms, Sir Percy?"

"Yes," he said, fishing out a slimy-looking lump. Before I could stop him he popped it in his mouth and chomped. "And very  tasty they are, too. If somewhat on the *chewy* side."

Whoops. It turned out I *hadn't* picked off all the slugs. *Ew.*

A couple of hours later, Patchcoat and I were sitting by the fire while Sir Percy dozed against a tree. He'd given us first watch, with strict instructions to wake him after two hours. The tiny fact that we had no way at all of telling the time didn't seem to bother him.

An owl hooted nearby, making us jump.

"I dunno about you, Ced, but I'll be glad to be out of this forest!" said Patchcoat.

"Me, too," I said. "Do you think anyone is missing us back at the castle?"

"Doubt it," said Patchcoat. "Sir Percy never said how long his hunt for the Ghost was going to take. Not that he had any *intention* of doing any actual hunting, of course."

I sighed. "So we could be lost in the forest for a *week* before anyone misses us."

"Or a month," said Patchcoat. "Or a year, even."

"Thanks, Patchcoat," I said. "That's really cheered me up."

"Look on the bright side, Ced," he grinned. "After a year of dock-and-slug soup, Margaret's porridge will taste like a royal banquet!"

He chuckled to himself and stretched out next to the fire. I tossed a couple more branches on to the flames.

"I reckon it's time to wake Sir Percy now, don't you?" I said.

But Patchcoat had nodded off. I went to my master and gently shook his shoulder.

71

"Nnnng! Eh? Wha…" he grunted, half opening an eye. "BEARS! HELP! HELP!"

"It's only me, Sir Percy," I said. "It's your turn to keep watch."

"Eh? What? Yes, yes, all right," he said, his head lolling forward on to his chest once more. "Hmmnnnninaminute." He closed his eyes and started to snore.

I tried shaking his shoulder again but he just snored more loudly. *Suspiciously* loudly.

"Great," I sighed. "It looks like I'll be staying up all night."

I decided to walk around a bit to try and keep myself awake, but I soon turned back. Even just beyond the firelight the forest was so dark I couldn't see a thing.

I was returning to the others when something flapped past my face.

"Yikes!" I was so startled that I lost my balance and tumbled into some bracken. "Bloomin' bats!" I muttered.

As I got to my feet, I spotted a gleam of light in the distance. Funny, I didn't think I'd wandered so far from the fire. But then I saw another gleam – and another, and another! They looked like torches. But whose? Maybe it was a search party! I had to tell the others.

I swung round and soon spotted our campfire. But then I froze. Two hooded figures were creeping into our camp!

Chapter Five

The Ghost's Gang

I watched as the figures pounced on
Patchcoat and Sir Percy. There were only
two of them – could we fight them off?
I started to run – then someone seized
me from behind.

"Not so fast, sonny!" said a gruff voice.

"Eek!" I cried, as strong arms grabbed
me firmly round the waist and lifted

me off my feet. Before I knew what was happening I was being carried into the firelight like a rolled-up rug.

"Look, Maud," chortled my captor, whose face was also hidden by a hood. "I've caught the little 'un!"

He plonked me down next to Sir Percy and Patchcoat, and waggled the heavy staff he was holding in his other hand. "Any more tricks like that an' he'll feel the Walloper on his backside!"

"Steady on, Jack," said the one he'd called Maud. "We don't want to terrify the poor lad."

"What the blazes is going on?" demanded my master. "Release me at once.

KNIGHTMARE

Do you know who I am?"

"Oh, we know who *you* are all right,"
Maud replied. "You're that bloke who's
been hunting the Ghost of Grimwood!"

Sir Percy's furious face switched
instantly to his most charming smile.

"Er, *who*, my dear lady?" he said.
"The *Ghost*? Never heard of him. We are –
um – simple travellers, lost in the forest."

"Travellers, eh?" said Maud. "So you're *not* a knight and his sidekicks, sent by the sheriff to catch the Ghost?"

"Good gracious, *no*!" smarmed Sir Percy. "Not at all! Perish the thought! Whatever gave you *that* ridiculous idea?"

"Well, for one thing you're wearing *armour*," said the woman. "And for another you left the sheriff's castle this morning. Ain't that right, Billy?"

"That's right," said a gangly youth. "Jack and me follered them out of town."

Then I remembered – Billy and Jack must have been the two peasants I'd noticed on the road!

"And we saw them take our secret forest

77

track," said Jack. "Not even my scary sign put them off. And if that wasn't bad enough, you tricked me when I tried to show you the way back to the castle."

"What?" said Sir Percy. "My dear sir, I have never set eyes on you in my life!"

"I was in disguise," said Jack. "I thought I'd fooled you with that false beard and my story about a man-eating monster."

"The tree hermit!" I gasped. "That was you!"

"You even pretended to sound terrified," Jack went on. "So once I'd shown you the quick way out of the forest, I took a shortcut back to my friends here and told them I'd seen you off. But it turns out you'd just ignored me and carried on towards our secret hideout. A clever trick!"

"Secret hideout?" said Sir Percy. "I assure you we had no idea we were anywhere near it!"

Or indeed where we were at all, I thought.

"A likely story," said Maud. "Later on I went fishing in the stream and spotted your fire. A bit too close to our hideout for comfort. I bet you were planning to sneak up on us when we were asleep. So I hurried off to fetch the others. And here we all are."

"I take my hat off to you, Sir Knight,"

said Jack. "You're obviously rather cunning. Unlike *most* of the sheriff's henchmen, eh, gang?"

The outlaws laughed.

"But my dear fellow, we are *not* friends of the sheriff's," insisted Sir Percy. "If you must know, it was the king who sent us into the forest."

"The king?" said Maud. "Well, we're certainly not enemies with *him*. Good bloke, the king is. All right, let's suppose you're being honest. Just tell me one thing. How did you know where to find our hideout?"

"We didn't," I chipped in. "We were chased off the path by a bear!"

"Very funny," said Jack. "Only there

ain't any bears in this part of the forest."

"And we should know, 'cause we *live* here," said Billy.

"But it's true!" said Patchcoat.

"Nice try, gents," sighed Maud. "Anyway, now we've captured you I'm afraid there's only one thing to do."

Eek! My heart skipped a beat.

"M-m-m-m-my dear madam!" jabbered Sir Percy. "N-n-n-now I do hope you're not planning anything *rash*!"

"We're going to take you back to the road," said Maud. "But only if you promise never to return. And we'll have to blindfold you. We don't want anyone sneaking back with the sheriff and his cronies."

"Oh, we promise, madam!" said
Sir Percy with a little giggle of relief.
"Knight's honour! Eh, chaps?"

Patchcoat and I nodded eagerly.

"Phew!" said Sir Percy. "You had me
worried there for a moment. I thought you
were going to, you know – beat us up. Or
worse."

The outlaws looked shocked.

"What a horrible idea!" exclaimed
Billy. "We'd never do such a thing!"

"Last night a peasant was robbed in
the forest," I said. "He was treated a bit
roughly. The sheriff blamed the Ghost."

"That's not our style at all," said
Maud. "We may be outlaws but we're not

baddies. We would never harm anyone!"

"'Cept p'raps the sheriff!" chuckled Jack. "He's the villain, not us!"

"That's right," said Billy. "We never robs anyone as can't afford it!"

"And we're always *really* polite," said Maud. "The Ghost insists on it. Speaking of being polite, allow us to introduce ourselves." She lowered her hood. "I'm Matron Maud, the Ghost's second-in-command."

As she stepped forward I saw that she was wearing a sword under her cloak and something told me she wasn't afraid to use it.

"I'm Lanky Jack," grinned Jack,

pushing back his hood. His bright beady eyes glinted in the firelight as he waved his staff under my nose. "Watch out for the Walloper!"

"I'm Billy Brown, the Boy with the Bow," said the skinny youth. As he lowered his hood, I was surprised to discover that he wasn't much older than me. I noticed rather enviously that he was carrying his own bow and arrows.

"And what about the Ghost?" said Sir Percy. "Where is he?"

"Oh, he's busy tonight," said Maud. "Let's just say he has an *appointment* with one of the sheriff's pals. A certain abbot with a large collection of gold rings. He'll be back in the morning."

"Talking of morning, it's nearly dawn," said Jack. "Time to blindfold these gentlemen and take them out of the forest. You first, Sir Knight."

Sir Percy stood up and allowed Jack to blindfold him. "No peeking!" smiled Jack. He then turned to me. "You next, sonny."

I suddenly remembered something. "By the way," I said. "I spotted your torches when you were sneaking up on us earlier."

"Torches?" said Maud. "What torches? We didn't have any torches."

"Well, if they weren't *your* torches, whose were they?" I asked.

Out of the darkness came the answer.

"They were *ours*!" barked a voice. "Stay wight where you are. I have you completely suwwounded!"

The outlaws gasped in horror as into the firelight strode the sheriff with Lurk, and half a dozen soldiers armed with pikes and crossbows.

"Excellent!" declared the sheriff. "Now I can keep that fat weward! I have captured the Ghost myself!"

"The Ghost isn't here," said Billy. "And you'll *never* catch him either, so there!"

"Shall I clobber 'im, sir?" said Lurk.

"You'll have to clobber me first!" said Maud, stepping forward.

"Don't bother," sneered the sheriff. "The boy's attempt to defend his leader is quite pathetic. *Not here* indeed. Ha! Just wait till the king learns that the Ghost is the *vewy* same knight who volunteewed to twack him down!"

He stepped up to Sir Percy and whipped off his blindfold.

"You can't hide behind that widiculous mask any more!" the sheriff cried in triumph. "Sir Percy, you are under awwest!"

Chapter Six

Stocks Shock

"I thought there was something fishy about you fwom the start," said the sheriff. "And then when I heard you wefuse the king's offer of troops I knew something was up. I'll bet you planned to hang about in the fowest for a bit, then go back to the king and pwetend you hadn't been able to find the Ghost. A cunning plan, Sir Percy.

Extwemely cunning. But not cunning enough!"

"Now look here, you've got it all wrong, old chap," said Sir Percy, ignoring the fact that the sheriff had actually got *most* of it right. "I'm really not the Ghost, you know."

"Nonsense!" snarled the sheriff. "I decided to miss the king's boar hunt and do some hunting of my own – for you, Sir Percy! If my hunch was cowwect, you and your two sidekicks would lead me stwaight to your gang. It was easy to find where you'd left the road and entered the fowest. All we did was follow your twacks. We found the spot where you cunningly left the path — but by then the sun had set and we lost your twail in the dark. I admit I was quite close to giving up — until I spotted your fire! We instantly put out our torches and cwept up on you. Heh, heh, heh! Oooh, I am so bwilliant!"

"But Sir Percy's telling the truth!" said Maud. "He isn't the real Ghost."

"Silence!" shrieked the sheriff. "Men, tie these wogues up. We're taking them back to the castle."

The sheriff's men roped us all together in a long line, with Sir Percy in front. I couldn't see Patchcoat but I guessed he was right at the back. Then they marched us through the forest at a cracking pace.

KNIGHTMARE

For one thing it was nearly daylight and easier to see where we were going. For another, whenever anyone slowed down, Lurk gave them a painful prod in the posterior with his spear. But the main reason we made such good progress was that the sheriff took us along various hidden tracks and paths.

"He seems to know this bit of Grimwood amazingly well," whispered Billy behind me.

"No whispewing!" bawled the sheriff, raising his hand to bring us to a halt. "I won't have you wascals plotting to escape! No speaking from now on, is that clear?"

Lurk cracked his hairy knuckles menacingly. None of us spoke.

"You insolent wuffians!" screeched the sheriff. "How dare you wefuse to answer me?"

Billy cleared his throat. "Um – because you told us not to speak," he said. The other outlaws tried not to smile.

The sheriff peered at Billy suspiciously.

"Humph," he snorted. "Good. Keep it that way. Now move it!"

We walked on. The sun had risen now and was glinting on Sir Percy's armour. Maud was behind him, followed by me, Billy and Lanky Jack bringing up the rear. It was then that I realized something.

Where was Patchcoat?

The sheriff's men marched us through the town gates and into the market square in front of Fleecingham Castle. The market was already under way, and people stopped to point and stare as we passed.

"'Ere, Mum, ain't that Sir Percy the

Proud?" said a peasant girl carrying a big basket of apples.

"Why, I do believe it is, Aggie dear," said her mum "What's 'e doin' all trussed up like a chicken?"

At the mention of Sir Percy's name people began to cluster around my master. One peasant ran forward with a quill pen and a dog-eared copy of *The Song of Percy*.

"Can I have yer autograph, Sir Percy?" he asked.

Sir Percy smiled wanly. "My dear fellow, I'd be delighted," he said. "But I'm afraid I'm rather tied up at the moment."

"Silence!" snapped the sheriff. "No fwaternizing with the pwisoners!"

"Prisoner?" said the peasant. "Why's Sir Percy a prisoner?"

"Because he's a dangewous cwiminal!" said the sheriff. He puffed up his chest and paused for dramatic effect. "He is the Ghost of Gwimwood!"

The stunned crowd stared at my master. The sheriff chuckled smugly and twiddled his moustache. And then someone broke the silence.

"Hooray for the Ghost! 'E's the friend of the poor!"

Then the whole crowd erupted.

"Good old Sir Percy!"

"We love you, Sir Percy!"

"Our hero!"

"SILENCE!" shrieked the sheriff. "Any more cheewing and I'll put your taxes up!"

"The king won't let you!" called a voice at the back of the crowd. Everyone looked to see who had spoken. Standing on a cart was a short peasant. He was wearing a hood pulled down over his eyes so I couldn't see his face, but I was sure there was something familiar about his voice.

"Insolent peasant!" the sheriff bawled. "Guards, awwest that man!"

Quick as a flash, the peasant jumped down from the cart and disappeared into the crowd.

"I am sure the king will let me do *whatever* I please when he knows I've caught the Ghost!" the sheriff went on. "He'll be so thwilled he'll offer me anything I want as a weward. And do you know what I'll ask for? A nice little bunch of *executions.* Starting with the Ghost and his gang! Heh, heh, heh!" he laughed madly. "Lurk, fetch His Majesty at once!"

"'E ain't 'ere, mister," said the girl with the apples. "'E's gone out huntin' again!"

"Too bad," said the sheriff, though he didn't look unhappy. "I'll have to have the executions without him. But while we get evewything weady I know exactly what to do with the pwisoners. Lurk, lock them in the stocks!"

Without further ado we were marched to the side of the square where the town stocks stood. Nothing unusual about that – every town has a set or two for folks who get into trouble with the law. But Fleecingham had about *ten* sets. And most of them looked new.

The sheriff's men untied us, and then Lurk clapped us in the stocks one by one.

"Why so many stocks?" I asked when it

was my turn.

"Sheriff's orders," grunted Lurk, unlocking a padlock with one of a large bunch of keys at his waist. "He likes to make an example of them that won't pay their taxes. Now stick yer head and hands in there."

He clapped the stocks over my neck and wrists, padlocked it shut and moved on to Lanky Jack.

"The last sheriff never shut *anyone* in the stocks," said Maud, once Lurk had finished. "He said it was humiliating. Good man, Sir Edward was."

"Really?" I said, surprised. "I thought he was a traitor?"

KNIGHTMARE

"No!" said Maud. "Sir Edward was one of the king's most loyal knights!"

"But what about the letter that showed he was plotting to overthrow the king?" I said.

"Probably a forgery," said Jack.

I was still puzzled.

"But if Sir Edward was such a good bloke, who would do such a mean thing?"

"We has our suspicions," said Jack. "Sir Edward's deputy was an earl. That's even posher than a knight. We reckon he were jealous and wanted Sir Edward's job for himself."

"We reckon the deputy forged the letter," said Maud. "We can't prove it but it certainly worked. Once Sir Edward had fled, the deputy got his job."

I gasped. "So Sir Edward's deputy was the sheriff!"

"That's right," said Jack. "Earl Crawleigh de Creepes himself."

Just then, the sheriff stepped forward to address the crowd. While Lurk had been locking us up, the sheriff had been ordering his men about. A couple of them had scuttled off into the market and now returned with bowls of eggs and several baskets of rotten vegetables.

"People of Fleecingham, feel fwee to hurl as many mouldy cabbages and wotten eggs as you like at the pwisoners!

KNIGHTMARE

In the meantime I've got to sort out a little bit of *chopping*, heh, heh!"

With a mad cackle the sheriff stomped off into the castle, leaving Lurk and a few guards to keep an eye on us.

I watched with dread as the crowd moved towards us. Any second now they would start calling us rude names and chucking nasty stuff at us. Sure enough, a particularly fierce-looking peasant stepped right up to me.

But to my surprise he said, "Bad luck, sonny! Sorry they caught you!"

He gave me a friendly pat on the head and wandered off. I looked at the others and saw that the same thing was

happening to them. Instead of being rude
and throwing rotten eggs and veg, the
crowd was treating the outlaws like heroes
– to the obvious annoyance of Lurk.

Sir Percy got the most fuss of all. Peasants shook his hand and said, "Good old Ghost!" Kindly old ladies fed him buns and tarts. In fact, Sir Percy soon began to enjoy the attention a little too much. When one man praised him for a particularly daring raid on the sheriff's tax collectors, my master just smiled and said, "Oh, it was nothing, old boy. One must stick up for the common people, you know!"

"Sir Percy!" I hissed. "You're not *actually* the Ghost, remember!"

"Oh, don't be such a spoilsport, Cedric," he said. "It's only a bit of harmless fun."

Trying not to sound rude, I pointed out that his bit of harmless fun might lose him his head.

"Don't worry, lad," said Jack. "You forget that the real Ghost is still free. Once he hears what's happened he's bound to rescue us!"

"That's right," said Maud, who was in the stocks beside Jack. "All we have to do is sit tight. Not that we've much choice. At least no one's chucking muck at us."

But Maud spoke too soon. At that moment a horse and cart trundled out through the castle gates. It was laden to the brim with what looked like a week's worth of poop from the castle stables. As the cart moved slowly over the drawbridge, I heard a horribly familiar voice.

KNIGHTMARE

"Blistering breastplates! As if it isn't bad enough missing *another* day's boar hunting, I have to get stuck behind a stinking stack of manure! Get a move on, dung-cart driver!"

My heart sank. Following the dung cart out of the castle were Sir Roland and Walter!

Chapter Seven

Mucking and Diving

Walter squealed with glee. "Look, Sir Roland!" he cried. "It's Sir Percy and Fatbottom!"

Uh-oh, here comes trouble, I thought, as Sir Roland and Walter strode over to Lurk.

"What's going on?" Sir Roland said. "The sheriff told me he'd caught the Ghost and his gang. So why's that pompous twit

Sir Percy in the stocks?"

"Sir Percy *is* the Ghost, Yer Honour,"
said Lurk. "He's a dangerous villain!"

"Percy? A dangerous villain?" Sir
Roland roared with laughter. "He's about
as dangerous as a bowl of porridge!"

(Actually that made Sir Percy sound
pretty scary. Sir Roland had clearly never
tried Mouldybun Margaret's porridge.)

"Ooh no, Yer Honour," said Lurk.
"He's had you fooled all along. He's a
master o' disguise, yer see."

"A master of disguise? Don't be ridic—"
Sir Roland suddenly stopped. "Hold on,
though. He *did* sneak into a princess's
castle in disguise… Hmm. I'm not likely

to forget *that* little episode in a hurry." He glowered at Sir Percy. "I don't think I ever got you back for that, did I, Percy?"

Sir Percy smiled weakly. "Now, now, Roly old chap," he said. "Let bygones be bygones, eh?"

"Can I throw a rotten cabbage at Fatbottom, Sir Roland?" asked Walter.

"A *cabbage*?" said Sir Roland, with a wicked twinkle in his eye. "Oh no, Walter. I've got a much better idea, hur-hur." He turned and bawled across the square. "Hey you! Dung-cart driver! Wait!"

The dung merchant had stopped nearby to let a cartload of timber go past. He looked rather startled – but then Sir

Roland shouting at the top of his voice would probably have startled a statue.

Sir Roland grabbed an empty basket from a nearby stall and thrust it into Walter's hands.

"Walter, take this to that dung cart and fill it up," he ordered.

"Who *me*, Sir Roland?"

"Yes, *you*!"

"With *poo*?"

"Yes, *poo*!" said Sir Roland. "And be quick about it!"

Walter reluctantly took the basket to the dung cart. I couldn't help laughing at the sight of him staggering back with a stinky basket of horse manure that he'd

KNIGHTMARE

just filled with his bare hands. But I wasn't laughing for long.

"Right, Walter," said Roland, scooping out a handful of manure. "Let 'em have it!"

"I say, Roland," said Sir Percy in alarm. "Surely you're not going to— *Aargh!*"

Sir Roland hurled a big dollop of doo-doo that hit my master in the face with a loud SPLAT!

"That'll teach you to make a fool of me,

Percy!" jeered Sir Roland.

"Your turn next, Fatbottom!" sneered
Walter.

I tried to dodge out of the way, but it
was impossible to move. SPLOP! – my
nose took a direct hit.

"Hey, Percy, how are you doing?"
laughed Sir Roland, landing another
manky missile on my master's head.
"You look a bit pooped!"

They carried on pelting us with poo
until the basket was empty. While Walter
was off fetching another load, I saw that
a cart of timber had stopped next to the
stocks and the sheriff had returned with
several workmen to unload it. They began
to build some sort of raised platform.
It looked like the stage for a travelling
show – until I saw two of the sheriff's men
lugging a fat wooden block off the back of
the cart.

Uh-oh. I'd seen one of those blocks
before, all covered in cobwebs in the
dungeons of Castle Bombast. It was a
chopping block, and not the kind that
Mouldybun Margaret uses for chopping up

turnips. This chopping block was for *heads*!

While I was watching, another cart rolled up to the platform. It was carrying straw.

Lurk chuckled unpleasantly. "That's ter soak up all the *blood*!" he said.

Yikes!

Then the sheriff came over to the stocks, carrying a sheet of parchment and a quill. "Lurk, why don't you wun along and fetch your axe," he said. "While I tick evewyone off my *chopping* list, heh, heh!"

"Yes, Yer Honour!" said Lurk and lumbered off.

"Lurk's a good fellow," said the sheriff. "You could say he's a chip off the old *block*!"

115

"I wish the Ghost would hurry up and rescue us!" I whispered to Jack.

"Me, too," said Jack. "I'm not sure I can take any more of the sheriff's terrible jokes."

Speaking of bad jokes, I wondered what had happened to Patchcoat.

Just at that moment, Lurk returned with a large and rather nasty-looking axe. And to make things worse, Walter was on his way back with a fresh basketful of poop. But he was having a job pushing through the growing crowd of onlookers.

Among them was the short peasant with the hood pulled over his eyes, who had called out earlier. I watched as he sidled over to a big heap of straw that had just been unloaded from the cart. Checking to see no one was looking, he quickly took something out of his pocket and knelt beside the heap. After a few seconds he disappeared back into the crowd.

The sheriff was still ticking us off his list. "Wight then, who's necks?" he said. "Geddit? *Necks*? Heh, heh, heh!"

"FIRE! FIRE!" one of the sheriff's guards suddenly cried out.

Flames licked at the heap of straw. Within seconds the crowd started running to get away from the great clouds of smoke that filled the air.

"Well, don't just stand there, you

mowons!" the sheriff barked to his guards. "Put it out before it spweads to the platform! Lurk, give those fools a hand to fetch water. And move that blasted stwaw cart before the whole lot catches!"

"Yes, Yer Honour!" said Lurk. Still clutching his axe, he ran off – and barged straight into the hooded peasant. They both tumbled to the ground.

"Idiot!" grunted Lurk, getting to his feet. "Mind where you're goin'!"

"Beg pardon!" said the peasant.

As Lurk lurched off into the smoke, I was surprised when the peasant ran up to *me*. But not half as surprised as I was when he pushed back his hood to reveal…

KNIGHTMARE

"Patchcoat!"

"At your service, Ced," he grinned. "I thought I'd create a little distraction. Lucky I still had my tinderbox, eh? Now let's get you all out of these stocks."

"But how?" I said. "Lurk has got the keys!"

Patchcoat chuckled. "Not any more, he hasn't!" he said, holding up a fat bunch of keys.

KNIGHTMARE

"Patchcoat, you're a genius!" I said, as he fumbled through the keys for the one that fitted my padlock. Within seconds I was free. My wrists and neck were a bit stiff but there was no time to lose.

Under the cover of the smoke, we released the others one by one, while Patchcoat quickly explained how he'd slipped behind a tree when the sheriff had turned up. He'd found his way back to the road by following us at a distance.

Sir Percy was the last out of the stocks.

"Thank you," he said. "Now, Cedric, kindly fetch a handful of straw to wipe all this muck off my armour."

120

KNIGHTMARE

"No time for that, Sir Percy!" said
Maud. "We need to get out of here!"

Even as she spoke, the smoke cleared for
a moment and a voice hollered, "Sheriff,
the prisoners are escaping!"

"Run!" I yelled. "Lurk's spotted us!"

"Head for the city gate!" called Maud,
as we bolted across the market square,
dodging through stalls and peasants
hurrying the other way with buckets of
water.

"Stop them!" roared the sheriff.

We weren't far from the gates, but
we still had to get past the guards on
duty, and the sheriff's men were catching
up fast. Then I spotted the straw cart.

The driver was nowhere to be seen – he'd probably gone to help put out the blaze. An idea flashed into my head.

"I know!" I said. "Hide in the straw cart!"

"Good thinking, lad!" said Maud. "Jack, you drive."

We clambered on to the cart and dived under the straw. My plan was working brilliantly. But hold on – where was Sir Percy?

I heard a sudden cry nearby and popped up from the straw to see my master sprawling in a collapsed pile of baskets. He obviously hadn't spotted the basket-seller's stall in the smoke.

KNIGHTMARE

"Over here, Sir Percy!" I shouted. "Hurry!"

Sir Percy got up and tried to run for it. But he had a basket stuck on his head and the basket seller wasn't keen to part with it.

"Stop! Thief! 'E's nicking one o' me baskets!" she hollered. She did an impressive dive and clasped Sir Percy's left leg.

"My good woman, kindly let go!"

"Not until you gimme back that basket!"

A cloud of smoke hid them from view. And then I heard a horribly familiar whiny voice.

"Fatbottom!" It was Walter, still carrying his basket of poop. "Trying to escape, eh? We'll soon see about that!" He plonked down the basket and jumped on to the cart.

"Gerroff, Wartface!" I cried, as he grabbed hold of me.

Jack was already in the driver's seat and saw what was happening. With a crack of the reins he cried, "Giddy up,

124

Dobbin!" and the cart lurched forward.

Walter lost his balance and loosened his grip just enough for me to give him a well-aimed kick in the shoulder.

"Waah!" he wailed, disappearing over the side of the cart.

I quickly checked to make sure he wasn't going to try again. I needn't have worried. He had tumbled off the cart head first into his basket of poop. *Ew.*

I dived back under the straw and we all lay very still as the cart trundled through the town gates, just as the church clock struck midday.

Close by, I heard the sheriff shouting to his men. "What do you mean, *vanished?*"

he raged. "Impossible! Search the town, you bwainless boobies!"

Tee-hee! I thought. *We did it!*

But then the sheriff spoke again. "At least they didn't all escape. We still have the most important pwisoner – the Ghost!"

I'd forgotten about Sir Percy! I dared to peek out of the straw one last time. There was my master, standing by the basket-seller's stall, his arms firmly held by two guards. He still had the basket on his head.

"That widiculous attempt at a disguise didn't fool anyone, Sir Percy!" snarled the sheriff. "Even if we can't catch the others, at two o'clock you will be executed!"

Chapter Eight
Royal Rescue

I guessed it wouldn't be long before Walter blabbed to the sheriff about how we'd made our getaway. So as soon as we reached the forest, we leaped from the cart and headed into the trees. Sure enough, we could already hear the sound of galloping hooves coming from the direction of the town.

"The sheriff will never find us in the

forest," said Maud. "We know lots of secret paths. Come on!"

Maud and the outlaws led the way along an unfamiliar track.

"Where are we going?" I asked.

"Our secret hideout," said Maud. "We never normally let strangers come near it. But I think you and Master Patchcoat have earned our trust, eh, lads?"

The other outlaws happily agreed.

"Once we're at the hideout we'll work out a way to save your master," Maud went on.

After half an hour or so we stopped to rest. I flopped down gratefully against a tree. I'd gone for a whole night without sleep and it had been ages since any of us had eaten properly. The only thing that stopped me dropping off was my grumbling tummy.

"I'll show you that new juggling trick again," said Patchcoat. "It'll take our minds off food." He rummaged in his pocket. "Bother. I seem to have lost one of my juggling balls. I wonder where—"

"Shh!" Billy suddenly put his fingers to his lips. "What's that sound?"

"*Voices!*" hissed Maud. "Coming this way!"

Sure enough, we caught the glint of metal through the trees.

"The sheriff's men!" said Billy. "How did

129

they know which way we came?"

"Dunno," said Jack. "But I ain't waiting around to find out. Down here, quick!"

We scrambled off the track down a rocky bank and picked our way through mossy boulders until the track was well out of sight. It was then that I saw a dark, narrow opening almost hidden among the rocks and trees.

"Hey, a cave!" I said. "We can hide in there until the coast is clear."

One by one we ducked into the narrow entrance. While the outlaws kept a lookout, Patchcoat and I explored the cave to see if there was another way out. As our eyes got used to the dim light we saw that it was actually much bigger than it looked. And then we saw something that made our hair stand on end. A bear!

We froze.

The bear appeared to be standing up, ready to pounce – but then nothing happened.

"Hold on," said Patchcoat. "There's something fishy going on here."

He walked coolly up to the bear, and lifted it off the wall!

"Look, Ced!" he laughed. "It's only a costume!"

I sighed with relief. And then something else caught my eye. Piled up near the bear costume were dozens of bulging sacks.

KNIGHTMARE

"What's all this?" I said.

I tried to pick up one of the sacks, but it was surprisingly heavy and slipped from my fingers. It fell on to the floor of the cavern, spilling its contents. I gasped in amazement. What tumbled out wasn't grain or flour but … coins! Bright, shiny gold and silver coins.

KNIGHTMARE

The outlaws came running up.

"Phew!" said Maud. "Where's this lot come from, then?"

"It looks like someone's secret stash of *loot*," I said. "Someone who's a famous *robber*, maybe?"

Patchcoat held up the bear costume. "Yeah, and a robber who's a *master of disguise* and likes to scare people off if they get too close! *Raahh!*"

"Aha! So there *was* a bear," said Jack. "But not a real one. Sorry for not believing you."

"Hold on," I said. "Are you saying this loot has nothing to do with you?"

"No way," said Jack, picking up the

empty sack. "This is tax money. Look."

He pointed to the words on the side of the sack.

Taxes
Property of H.M. the King.
HANDS OFF!

"Tax money?" I said. "Doesn't that belong to the sheriff?"

"Oh no. It belongs to the king," said Maud. "The sheriff only collects it. He keeps it all locked up at the castle until the king's men come for it."

"We'd never steal off the king," added Billy.

KNIGHTMARE

"So you're saying someone stole this from the castle?" I said. "From right under the sheriff's nose?"

"That's right," said Jack. "Though I don't see how. The sheriff's men guard it day and night."

"Hmm," I said. "Unless the thief is ... the sheriff himself?"

"Vewy clever, boy," said an icy voice. "Vewy clever indeed. But not clever enough. You're all under awwest. And this time you won't escape!"

"How did you know which way we'd come?" said Maud.

KNIGHTMARE

The sheriff's men had dragged us outside the cave and were busily tying us up.

"Easy," smirked the sheriff. "We weren't sure which path to take. But then we found *this*."

He held up Patchcot's missing juggling ball.

"Whoops," said Patchcoat. "Sorry, guys."

"So, you found my little nest egg, eh?" said the sheriff. "Of course, I send the king *most* of the taxes I take off those stupid peasants. But I think it's nice to put a little aside for a wainy day, don't you?"

"But you're cheating the king!"

I blurted. "That's treason!"

"Tweason shmeason," smirked the
sheriff. "The king is never going to find
out about the stolen taxes. And if he does,
I'll just blame the Ghost. Like with that
peasant you wobbed the other night, eh,
boys? The Ghost may be a hewo now,
but a few more stunts like that and the
peasants will soon change their tune."

His henchmen laughed nastily.

"The king will never believe you!"
said Billy.

"Won't believe me, eh?" snarled the
sheriff. "Well, if he was stupid enough
to believe the forged letter that got Sir
Worthington sacked, he'll believe anything!

KNIGHTMARE

Mind you, it was a rather *bwilliant* forgewy, if I say so myself! Heh, heh, heh!"

"So it *was* you!" said Maud. "But why? Why did you want the sheriff's job so badly?"

"So I could steal all this loot, of course!" said the sheriff. "And once I've stolen enough I shall be able to pay for my own army. Then I shall march out of Fleecingham, overthwow King Fwedbert and the kingdom will be mine, all mine! Hooway for King Cwawliegh the First!"

He threw his head back and let out a long, shrill cackle.

"You'll never get away with this!" I said. "We'll tell the king!"

KNIGHTMARE

"What?" the sheriff chortled. "Do you think the king will believe a boy, a jester and a bunch of outlaws? Especially when they haven't got any heads! Heh, heh, heh! I hope Lurk's axe is nice and sharp! Which weminds me, it's time to be heading back. Geddit? Be heading? Beheading? Heh, heh, heh! Men, bwing the pwisoners. Chop-chop! Geddit?"

THUNK!

An arrow landed right between the sheriff's feet. He squawked in fright and leaped into the arms of the nearest henchman.

I gasped as out of the trees rode … the king and queen! The queen was just notching another arrow to her bow.

"Nice shot!" said Billy.

"NOBODY MOVE!" boomed the king.
"We have you surrounded!"

With the king and queen were Sir
Spencer and Algernon, several other
knights and nobles, plus a bunch of royal
guards on foot.

KNIGHTMARE

"Well, well, well," said the king. "There we all were stalking a boar and instead we end up catching a rat! We've just overheard all your plans, sheriff. So, first you cheated Sir Edward out of his job and now you want mine, too, eh?"

The sheriff had gone rather pale. "But Y-y-your Majesty is mistaken!" he cringed. "Surely you didn't think that I would betway your woyal self, sire?"

"SILENCE!" blasted the king. "Sheriff, you and your henchmen are under arrest for treason, theft and forgery. Guards, seize them!"

Two royal guards stepped forward and took the sheriff by the arms, and then a

large and very cross wild boar suddenly
burst out of the bushes. It charged
straight through the king's guards and
archers, who scattered in alarm. The
sheriff's men grabbed their chance and
bolted through the gap. The sheriff
wriggled free of the royal guards and fled
into the trees as fast as his legs would
carry him.

"After them!" cried the queen.

"Blast that boar!" growled the king. "The next time I see it I jolly well hope it's on my dinner plate! Sir Spencer, stay here and guard the outlaws."

"M-me, sire?"

"Yes, you, you fool!" the king bellowed. "I'll deal with them later!"

The king and queen rode off, leaving us alone with Sir Spencer and Algernon. Sir Spencer eyed us nervously.

Then he noticed me. "Why, it's Percy's squire! I almost didn't recognize you under all that, er … muck. What are you doing here, young Frederick?"

"Cedric, Sir Spencer. It's a long story,"

I said. "But you have to help us. The sheriff is having Sir Percy executed at two o'clock!"

Out of the corner of my eye, I saw Billy slipping back into the cave. A few moments later he returned carrying something under his arm and dived behind a bush.

"But the king ordered me to stay here, Eric," Sir Spencer was saying. "I can't—"

ROAR!

A bear came lumbering towards us!

"Quick, Sir Spencer!" said Patchcoat. "Make for the cave while we distract it!"

Sir Spencer squealed and dived into the cave, with Algernon hot on his heels. Once they were out of sight the bear stopped roaring, and took off its head!

KNIGHTMARE

Billy grinned. "That bear costume did the trick!"

"Well done, Billy!" said Maud. "Cedric and Patchcoat, take the horses, quickly! We'll follow on foot."

Taking a knight's horse without permission is a total no-no, but this was an emergency. Within seconds I was riding back down the track, with Patchcoat trotting behind on Algernon's tubby pony.

We hadn't gone far when we heard Sir Spencer calling, "Hey! Where is everybody? And where's my horse?"

Explanations would have to wait. There was no time to lose. We had to save Sir Percy!

Chapter Nine
Chopper Stopper

A boy on a knight's warhorse looks rather suspicious, so Patchcoat and I dismounted well before the town gates and ran the last bit. We slipped through the gates among a crowd of peasants.

"You 'ere for the execution?" said an old man. "It's a shame they caught the Ghost and all that. But seein' how he's definitely a goner we might as well enjoy the show, eh?"

"There won't *be* any show if I can help it," I muttered. But how were we going to save Sir Percy? The church clock said ten to two.

"Programme, sonny?" croaked another peasant, thrusting a leaflet into my hand. "Only sixpence!"

Patchcoat and I glanced at the leaflet:

Souvenir Programme
Execution of Sir Percy a.k.a.
The Ghost of Grimwood
Order of events
2.00p.m. Sir Percy gets his
head chopped off.
2.01p.m. Everyone goes home.

I glared at the peasant and handed it back.

"That's terrible!" I said.

"Too right," said Patchcoat. "Sixpence is a rip-off!"

We reached the front of the crowd but there was no chance of getting any nearer to Sir Percy. The sheriff's men stood all around the platform, shoving back any onlookers who got too close. On the platform itself stood Sir Percy, guarded by two soldiers. Lurk was beside the chopping block, wearing a mask and sharpening his axe.

"Quite a big crowd, ain't it, Sir Percy?" Lurk said. "Must be a *block* booking. Muh-huh! 'Ere, 'ow does a Chinese executioner eat 'is dinner? With chopsticks. Muh-huh-huh!"

A ripple of titters ran through the square. Lurk winked at the crowd.

"I say, this just isn't on, you know," said Sir Percy. "You can't go chopping a chap's head off without the king's permission!"

"Well, the king ain't 'ere, is he?" growled Lurk. "Sorry, Sir Percy, sheriff's orders. It's nuffink personal. I haven't got an axe to grind. Except this one! Muh-huh! Now, no more arguing or I'll knock yer block off. Oh, silly me, I forgot. I'm goin' to knock yer block off anyway. Muh-huh-huh-huh!"

"We have to do something!" I said to Patchcoat. "And fast!"

Looking around the square in desperation, I noticed two things. First, the square was on a bit of a slope, with the castle at the higher end and the platform at the bottom. Second, all the castle guards had sneaked into the crowd to see the execution. The castle was totally unguarded. I had a sudden thought.

"Patchcoat, make for the castle!" I said.

"Eh?" said Patchcoat. "The king isn't
there, Ced!"

"But Sir Roland is!" I panted. "*He'll*
have to stop the execution! He can't hate
Sir Percy *that* much! Come on!"

We jostled our way out of the crowd and
sprinted across the square. We were already
on the drawbridge when I spotted the dung
cart. The dung merchant was nowhere to be
seen. He was probably in the crowd, too. I
had a flash of inspiration.

"You go and find Sir Roland!" I said.
"I've got an idea. Hurry!"

As Patchcoat scurried off into the castle
I ran to the cartload of dung.

I reached the cart and fumbled frantically with the horse's harness.

"Right, folks, it's almost showtime!" bawled Lurk. "This one's a real *block*buster, muh-huh-huh!"

"My good fellow, I insist that you release me at once," said Sir Percy. "I shan't ask you again!"

"Funny you should say that," grinned Lurk.

"That's it, Lurk, keep 'em coming!" I mumbled. Every joke he cracked gave me a few extra seconds to save my master.

At last I freed the horse from its harness and shooed it in the direction of a pile of juicy carrots on a nearby stall.

"What's up, Sir Percy?" quipped Lurk. "You look a bit pale. Got a headache? Don't worry, I've got the perfect cure! Muh-huh-huh!"

I ran to the back of the cart and gave it a shove. It didn't budge. My heart stopped as I saw the guards seizing Sir Percy by the arms.

I tried again. "One, two, three… HEAVE!"

At last the heavy cart began to move – slowly at first, then gathering speed as it trundled downhill.

The church clock struck two.

The dung cart was now hurtling out of control. Someone yelled, "Watch out!" and

then there was mayhem as people dived
out of the way.

"Right. Time to get yer head down, Sir
Percy," said Lurk, running his thumb along
the blade of his axe. "Before you know it
you'll be droppin' off! Muh-huh-h… Eh?
What? 'Ere! STOP THAT CART!"

But it was too late. Lurk could only
stand there gawping as the crowd parted,
the guards leaped for cover, and the dung
cart crashed into the platform with an
almighty CRRR-UNCH!

"Aargh!"

The cart shed its load and sent an
avalanche of steaming manure flying over
Lurk. I'd done it!

A moment later, there was another kerfuffle nearby and the royal hunting party rode into the square, with the sheriff and his henchmen as prisoners.

"Shivering shield-straps!" bellowed the king, seeing the platform. "Has someone ordered an execution? I can't stand executions. I'll have someone's head for this!"

Just then, Patchcoat came out of the castle accompanied by Sir Roland.

"Where are all the guards, Sir Roland?" demanded the queen. "You were supposed to be in charge of the castle while we were out hunting!"

"And you were supposed to keep order!" said the king, riding up. "The place is in chaos!"

"Er, well, I, er…" Sir Roland burbled sheepishly.

KNIGHTMARE

"The sheriff!" I cried. "He's getting away!"

While the guards had been distracted by the commotion in the square, the sheriff had managed to break free.

"I'm off!" he cackled and sprinted for the town gates.

"You bumbling bunch of beetle-brains!" seethed the king. "Somebody stop him!"

It looked like the sheriff would escape again, but then I spotted something.

"Up there, Your Majesties!" I shouted. "On the battlements!"

A figure was running along the top of the town walls towards the gates. It looked like the dung merchant. Except for one thing. He was wearing a mask.

"It's the Ghost of Grimwood!" said Patchcoat. "And look, here comes his gang!"

It was true. Hurrying through the town gates were Maud, Billy and Jack.

"Ahoy there, gang!" called the Ghost. "Don't let the sheriff escape!"

At once Jack and Billy ran back to the gates and heaved them shut.

"Blast and bothewation!" cried the sheriff.

He fled into the market stalls with his cloak flapping behind him. But he wasn't fast enough for Billy.

SWISH! THUNK!

KNIGHTMARE

A second later, one of Billy's arrows pinned the sheriff's cloak to a large barrel of apples.

"Good shot, Billy!" I cheered.

But in a trice the sheriff wriggled free of his cloak and sped off towards a nearby sewer. This was basically a large (and VERY smelly) trench that ran out of the town through a low arch in the walls.

"You fools!" he cackled, jumping into the sewer and splashing his way towards the arch. "I'm not finished yet!"

But neither was the Ghost.

The crowd *ooh*-ed and *aah*-ed as the Ghost leaped from the battlements on to the roof of a house, skated skilfully down the thatch, then somersaulted neatly on to a horse that was waiting to be hitched to a cartload of turnips.

"Yah!" cried the Ghost. "Go get'im, girl!"

The horse reared up, whinnied and galloped after the sheriff.

KNIGHTMARE

Riding with no hands, the Ghost unwound a rope from his waist, tied one end in a loop, swung it round his head, and neatly slipped it over the fleeing sheriff.

"Waah!" wailed the sheriff, as the loop tightened around his waist and arms. "Dwat and double-dwat!"

In one smooth move, the Ghost hauled the sheriff out of the sewer and on to the horse. Then he calmly trotted up to the king.

"Special delivery, sire," he said. "One rather stinky sheriff!"

"S-sire!" blustered the sheriff. "I can explain everything!"

KNIGHTMARE

But at that moment a poop-covered figure ran past us, making for the gates. It was Lurk.

"The deputy sheriff!" I said. "He's getting away!"

"Stop that man!" ordered the king.

Lurk had a head start on the royal guards. But he hadn't reckoned with Maud.

"Not so fast, sunshine!" she cried, and started bombarding him with apples from the barrel that still had the sheriff's cloak pinned to it.

"Aargh!" cried Lurk, as several well-aimed apples bounced off his head. He turned and ran back past us, but then Jack stuck out his staff and tripped him over. The royal guards instantly pounced on him and held him fast.

"To the dungeons with them!" said the king. "I'll think of a suitable punishment later. And I suppose I'll also need a new sheriff." He sighed. "I should never have believed that letter. I'd give Sir Edward his job back if I knew where he was."

"Actually, he's not very far away, sire," said the Ghost.

"Really?" said the king. "Where is he?"

The Ghost peeled off his mask to reveal a handsome face with piercing blue eyes.

"Here, sire," he said, cocking an eyebrow. He bowed deeply in his saddle. "Sir Edward Worthington, at your service."

KNIGHTMARE

There were gasps of astonishment.

"Great galloping gargoyles!" exclaimed the king. "Sir Edward. So you're the Ghost of Grimwood!"

"And the dung merchant," I piped up. His disguise had been very convincing. And, let's face it, most people avoided getting too close to a dung merchant if they could help it.

"Indeed," smiled Sir Edward. "I never fled abroad at all. That was just a story I spread so no one would suspect that I was the Ghost, hiding in the forest with my loyal followers."

The outlaws stepped forward, and bowed to the king and queen.

KNIGHTMARE

"I suspected the sheriff was behind the letter, but I couldn't prove it," Sir Edward continued. "The dung merchant's job was the perfect means of getting in and out of the castle to do a bit of spying. I didn't find out about the letter, but I overheard the sheriff telling Lurk to collect more and more tax off the peasants but *none at all* from the sheriff's rich cronies. I thought that wasn't right, sire. So I decided to – um – make things a bit fairer."

"By robbing the sheriff's wealthy friends?" frowned the king. "I see. Well, I don't really approve of stealing, you know, Sir Edward."

"Of course not, sire," said Sir Edward.

"But we didn't keep anything for ourselves. We gave it back to the peasants to make up for all the extra tax they were paying."

"Oh well, I *suppose* that's all right," said the king. "I shall be happy to say no more about it. If *you* will forgive *me* for believing that letter, Sir Edward."

"Of course, sire. It was very convincing," he said. "The sheriff was an excellent forger."

"And a thief!" said the king. "He was keeping some of my tax money and hiding it in a secret cave in the forest! Your gang came across it today."

"Actually, it was young Master Cedric who discovered it!" Maud piped up.

"Did he indeed?" beamed the king. "Good lad!"

I blushed. "Well, it was by accident really, Your Majesty," I said.

"*And* he saved Sir Percy," added Patchcoat.

"By the way, where is your master?" asked the king.

At that very moment there was a muffled groan from the platform. The mountain of manure appeared to be moving. Then a head popped up out of the stinky heap. It was Sir Percy.

"I say," he whimpered. "Will someone kindly get me out of here?"

KNIGHTMARE

A few hours later Patchcoat and I were in the stable yard preparing to leave. We had just hitched Gristle to the cart while Sir Percy stood nearby checking his armour in a downstairs window. You'd think the first thing you'd say to someone who'd *literally* just saved your neck was "Thanks!". But not Sir Percy. Once we'd hauled him out of the manure mountain he'd told me to fetch a cloth at once and clean the horse-poo off his armour. Oh well.

I was about to fetch Prancelot from her stall when the ex-outlaws arrived to say goodbye. Jack and Billy were both wearing smart coats of mail and scarlet tunics bearing Sir Edward's emblem, an eagle.

"What's with the fancy outfits?" said Patchcoat. "We almost didn't recognize you!"

"I used to be head of the castle guard," said Jack. "Till Earl Crawleigh de Creepes sacked me. Sir Worthington gave me my old job back. He's my boss now, along with the new deputy sheriff!"

"Deputy sheriff?" I said. "Who's that?"

"Me!" said Maud. "So this lot had better mind their Ps and Qs!"

The ex-outlaws all laughed.

Billy had his bow over his shoulder. He unslung it and handed it to me.

"This is for you," he smiled. "I saw you admiring it when we were in the forest."

"Really?" I gasped. "Are you sure?"

"Oh yes," he said. "I've got tons of bows now Sir Worthington's put me in charge of all his archers!"

I thanked Billy again. Then the ex-outlaws said goodbye and returned to the castle.

"Wow! My very own bow!" I said after they had gone. "I can't wait to try it out!"

Sir Percy came over from the window. "Right, chaps, I think we're ready," he said. "Cedric, fetch Prancelot and we'll be on our way."

"Yes, Sir Percy," I said. I put my bow on the seat of the mule cart and was about to step into the stables, when who should appear but the king.

"Ah, there you are, Sir Percy!" he boomed. "I was hoping to catch you before you left. All cleaned up now?"

"Yes, sire," said Sir Percy.

"Good! Otherwise we'd have to start calling you Sir Percy the Poop instead of Sir Percy the Proud, eh?" the king guffawed.

"Ha ha ha! *Most* amusing, sire!" winced Sir Percy. "Well, I suppose we must be off. Long journey home and all that!"

"Ah, good old Sir Percy," the king chortled. "You're such a joker!"

Sir Percy looked a bit bewildered. "Um – I am, sire?" he said.

"Come now, Sir Percy," the king chuckled. "As if you'd really try to leave without giving me … my *birthday present*?"

Sir Percy went pale. He looked about frantically. And then something caught his eye.

"Ah, there it is, sire!" he declared.

"Phew! I-I wondered where my squire had put it!"

My heart sank as Sir Percy reached over to the seat of the mule cart and picked up … my bow!

"Of course I-I knew Your Majesty must have one already, but … but it's always useful to have a spare, eh, sire!"

The king was delighted. "Quite so, Sir Percy, quite so!" he exclaimed. "Especially as I managed to snap mine while I was hunting. It's the perfect present. Now have a good journey home!"

And the king swept back into the castle, clutching the bow. *My* bow.

That's another one you owe me, Sir Percy!

Coming Soon!